Astronomy

Emily Bone
Designed by Matthew Preston and Sam Chandler
Illustrated by John Fox and Uta Bettzieche

Astronomy consultant: Dr. Leila Powell
Reading consultant: Alison Kelly

Contents

- 3 Studying the sky
- 4 What's in space?
- 6 A place in space
- 8 Watching space
- 10 Telescopes in space
- 12 Looking at galaxies
- 14 The Milky Way
- 16 Studying stars
- 18 The Sun
- 20 Probing planets
- 22 Exploring the surface
- 24 The Moon
- 26 Space lumps
- 28 Stargazing
- 30 Glossary
- 31 Internet links
- 32 Index

Studying the sky

When you look up at the night sky, you might see lots of stars. This is only a tiny part of space.

Astronomers study space to find out about the different things that are found there.

What's in space?

There are lots of different things in space.

Planets are big, round lumps of rock or balls of gases.

Some have rocky or icy moons moving around them.

Smaller pieces of rock or ice are called asteroids.

Stars are massive balls of gases. Many have planets moving around them.

Millions and millions of stars are grouped together in galaxies...

...and there are millions and millions of galaxies in space.

A place in space

Planet Earth is one of eight planets that move around a star called the Sun.

The Sun and planets are known as the Solar System.

The Sun

Mercury

Venus

Earth

Mars

Jupiter

The planets in the Solar System are very far apart. They're very different sizes, too.

Jupiter is the biggest planet. This is how big Jupiter is compared to Earth.

Jupiter is so far away from Earth, it looks like a bright star in the sky.

Saturn

Uranus

Neptune

Watching space

Astronomers use telescopes to get clear pictures of things that are in space. There are lots of different types of telescopes.

Radio telescopes find planets, stars and galaxies by collecting signals from space.

These are some of the ALMA radio telescopes in Chile, South America.

The Keck telescopes in Hawaii, U.S.A., use huge, curved mirrors and cameras to make pictures.

At night, light from a planet is reflected from the mirrors into the cameras.

The cameras turn this light into a clear picture of the planet.

Telescopes in space

Some telescopes fly around the Earth in space. The Hubble telescope is a famous space telescope.

Big mirrors on Hubble reflect light coming from distant galaxies.

A camera takes pictures of the galaxies and measures how far away they are.

Hubble sends signals to radio dishes on Earth. The dishes send signals to computers.

The computers turn the signals into pictures. This is a picture of the Antennae Galaxies, taken by Hubble.

Sometimes, astronauts have to go into space to fix Hubble.

Looking at galaxies

Astronomers have discovered different types of galaxies.

Some galaxies are shaped like a spiral. This picture of a spiral galaxy was taken by the Hubble telescope.

Other galaxies are known as irregular galaxies. These can be different shapes.

The Cartwheel Galaxy looks like a wheel.

Some galaxies are slowly joining together.

These two spiral galaxies will eventually become one even bigger galaxy.

The Milky Way

The Solar System is part of a galaxy known as the Milky Way.

Astronomers pointed the Spitzer space telescope at stars in the Milky Way.

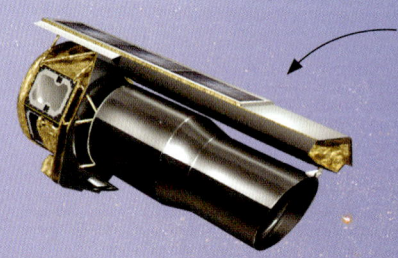

This is Spitzer. It's around the same size as Hubble.

A camera on Spitzer took pictures of different stars.

It sent this information to computers on Earth.

The computers used signals from Spitzer to make a big picture of the Milky Way.

The Solar System is around here.

Astonomers are looking for planets in the Milky Way outside our Solar System.

Studying stars

Stars form inside a swirling cloud of gas and dust, called a nebula.

Astronomers use telescopes to study how stars form.

This is a picture of the Carina Nebula taken by the Hubble space telescope.

The bright points of light inside the nebula are new stars.

 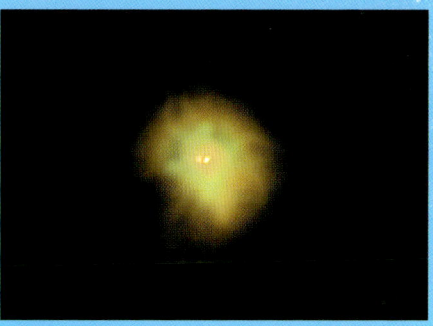

Gas and dust in part of the nebula start to form a clump. It gets hotter.

Gradually, the hot clump becomes a bright, glowing ball. This is a star.

 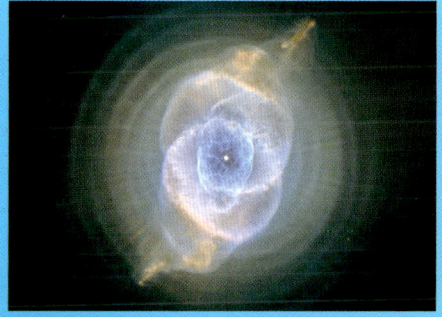

The star glows for millions of years. Slowly, it gets bigger and redder.

Eventually, layers of gas puff off into space, and the star fades away.

The biggest stars end in a huge explosion called a supernova.

The Sun

The Sun is the closest star to Earth. Astronomers study the Sun using the SOHO space telescope. It flies around the Sun in space.

SOHO took this picture of the Sun.

Never ever look directly at the Sun. Its strong light could hurt your eyes.

This is a close-up picture taken from SOHO of a huge loop of gas on the Sun.

SOHO blocks out the Sun's light to detect hot gas around the Sun, called a corona.

It also photographs sunspots, which are cooler patches on the Sun's surface.

Probing planets

A probe is a type of spacecraft that flies to planets. It takes lots of pictures and sends them back to computers on Earth.

This is a probe called Voyager 2. It took this picture of Neptune.

The probe found dark swirls on the planet. These are huge storms.

Venus is covered in thick clouds. The Magellan probe used signals to make pictures of the surface.

The Magellan probe sent signals through the clouds.

The signals bounced off the surface, then back up to the probe.

A computer used the signals to make this picture of the surface.

Exploring the surface

Rovers are vehicles that explore planets. They drive around, taking pictures of the surface and studying rocks.

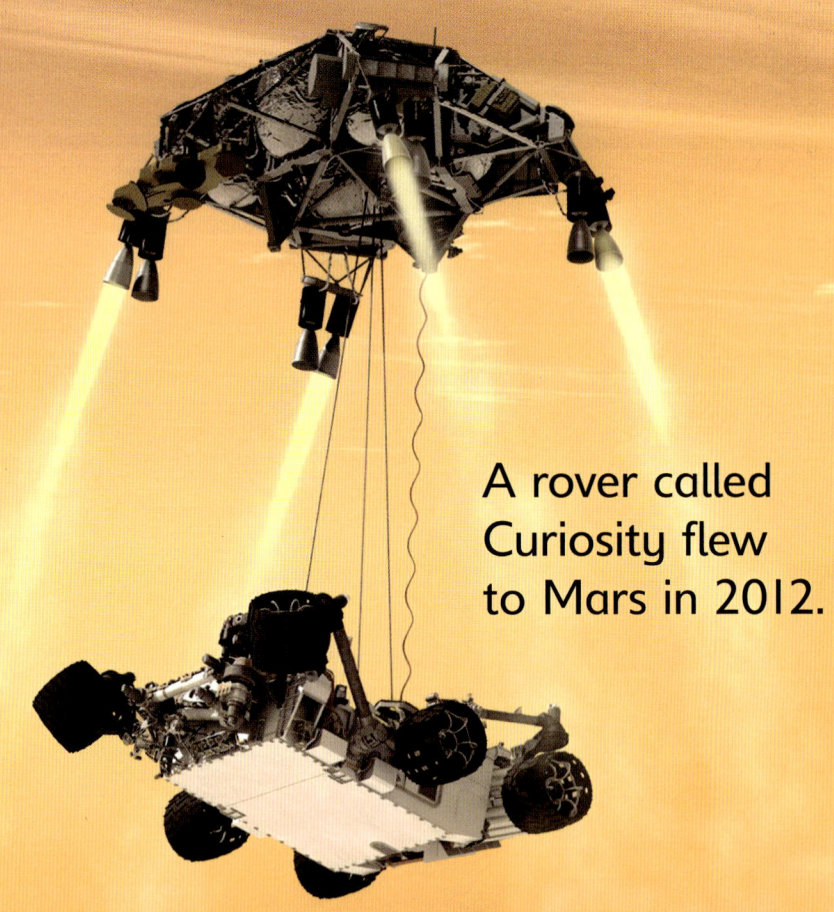

A rover called Curiosity flew to Mars in 2012.

This is how Curiosity looked as it was lowered to the surface by a spacecraft.

Curiosity has studied different rocks to look for signs of water.

Arm

A drill on the end of Curiosity's arm made a hole in a rock. This made lots of dust.

It moved its arm to scoop up dust, then tested it.

It sent the results of the tests back to astronomers on Earth.

The Moon

The Earth has a smaller, rocky ball moving around it, called the Moon.

As the Moon moves, the Sun lights up different parts of it, so it looks as though it's changing shape each night.

When you can only see a small part of the Moon, it's called a Crescent Moon.

For over 50 years, astronomers have used spacecraft to find out about the Moon.

In 1959, a Russian spacecraft flew around the Moon and took pictures.

Astronauts landed on the Moon in 1969. They took rocks back to Earth.

Astronomers sent a probe to the Moon to study its soil in 2009.

In the future, people might live on the Moon.

Space lumps

Asteroids are lumps of rock, ice or metal in space. Sometimes, they crash into Earth.

Some rocks heat up as they move close to the Earth.

They get hotter and hotter until they catch fire.

All the rock and metal burns up, leaving just a streak of light in the sky.

Other rocks don't burn up. They hit the Earth instead. Astronomers study them to find out about rocks in space.

This rock landed on Earth. It's shown here at around twice its actual size.

It's been cut open to see what's inside. The shiny pieces inside the rock are metal.

When some space rocks hit Earth, they make holes called craters.

Stargazing

You can see lots of different things in the night sky without using a telescope.

Some stars look like patterns in the sky. They are called constellations.

This constellation is Canis Major. If the stars are joined by lines, it looks like a dog.

Constellations can look different when you see them from different places on the Earth.

Sometimes, glowing lights appear in the sky. This is called an aurora.

A comet is a lump of dust and ice. It has a bright tail that can be seen from Earth.

The bright strip of stars in this picture is the middle of the Milky Way galaxy.

Glossary

Here are some of the words in this book you might not know. This page tells you what they mean.

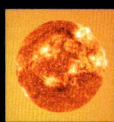 star - a huge ball of gases in space. The Sun is a star.

 galaxy - a group of millions and millions of stars.

 telescope - equipment that makes things that are far away seem larger.

 nebula - a swirling cloud of gas and dust where stars form.

 probe - a spacecraft for exploring planets that is controlled by a computer.

 rover - a computer-controlled vehicle that drives across a planet.

 constellation - stars in the night sky that look like a pattern.

Websites to visit

You can visit exciting websites to find out more about astronomy.

To visit these websites, go to the Usborne Quicklinks Website at **www.usborne-quicklinks.com**

Read the internet safety guidelines, and then type the keywords "**beginners astronomy**".

The websites are regularly reviewed and the links in Usborne Quicklinks are updated. However, Usborne Publishing is not responsible, and does not accept liability, for the content or availability of any website other than its own. We recommend that children are supervised while on the internet.

This is a picture of the Tycho Supernova taken by the Spitzer space telescope.

Index

aurora, 29
asteroids, 4, 26-27
astronauts, 11, 25
comets, 29
constellations, 28, 30
Earth, 6, 10, 23, 26, 27, 28, 29
galaxies, 5, 8, 10, 11, 12-13, 14, 15, 30
Milky Way, 14-15, 28-29
moons, 4, 24-25
nebula, 16, 17, 30
night sky, 3, 7, 9, 26, 28-29
planets, 4, 6, 7, 8, 9, 15, 20, 21, 22, 23
probes, 20-21, 25, 30
rovers, 22-23, 30
Solar System, 6-7, 14, 15
stars, 3, 4, 5, 6, 7, 8, 14, 16-17, 28, 29, 30
Sun, 6, 18-19, 24
supernova, 17, 31
telescopes, 8-9, 10-11, 12, 14, 16, 18, 19, 30

Acknowledgements

Photographic manipulation by John Russell

Photo credits

The publishers are grateful to the following for permission to reproduce material:
cover © **STScI/NASA** (Hubble space telescope); © **J. Hester, P. Scowen (ASU), HST, NASA** (Eagle Nebula); p1 © **NASA** (New Horizons space probe); p2-3 © **David Nunuk/Getty Images**; p4 © **NASA, ESA, and the Hubble Heritage Team (STScI/AURA)**; p5 © **the Hubble Heritage Team (AURA/ STScI/ NASA)** (galaxy); © **R. Williams (STScI), the Hubble Deep Field Team and NASA** (galaxy group); p6-7 © **Hubble Heritage Team, D. Gouliermis (MPI Heidelberg) et al., (STScI/AURA), ESA, NASA** (starry background); p6 © **SOHO (ESA & NASA)** (The Sun) © **Lunar and Planetary Institute** (Mercury); © **NASA/JPL** (Venus and Mars); © **NASA** (Earth); © **NASA/JPL/University of Arizona** (Jupiter); p7 © **NASA/JPL/STSI** (Saturn); © **William Radcliffe/Science Faction/Corbis** (Uranus); © **NASA** (Neptune); p8 © **Babak Tafreshi, TWAN/ Science Photo Library**; p9 © **Richard Wainscoat/Alamy** (Keck telescopes); © **NASA/JPL/University of Arizona** (Jupiter); p10 and 11 © **NASA, ESA, and the Hubble Heritage Team (STScI/AURA)-ESA/Hubble Collaboration**; p12 © **X-ray: NASA/CXC/Wisconsin/D.Pooley and CfA/A.Zezas; Optical: NASA/ESA/ CfA/A.Zezas; UV: NASA/JPL-Caltech/CfA/J.Huchra et al.; IR: NASA/JPL-Caltech/CfA**; p13 © **NASA/ JPL-Caltech** (irregular galaxy); © **NASA/JPL-Caltech/STScI/Vassar** (merging galaxy); p15 © **NASA/JPL-Caltech**; p16-17 © **NASA, ESA, and the Hubble SM4 ERO Team**; p17 © **NASA, ESA, HEIC, and The Hubble Heritage Team (STScI/AURA)**; p18, 19 © **NASA/SDO** (whole Sun and solar flare); p19 © **ESA/ NASA/epa/Corbis** (corona); © **SOHO/ESA/NASA/Science Photo Library** (sunspots); p20 © **NASA/JPL** (Neptune); © **NASA/JPL-Caltech** (Voyager 2 probe); p21 © **NASA/JPL** (Venus surface probe step); © **NASA/ JPL**; p22 © **NASA**; p23 © **NASA/JPL-Caltech/Science Photo Library**; p24 © **NASA/GSFC-SVS/Science Photo Library**; p25 © **NASA Images/Alamy** (astronaut on Moon); p26 © **Thomas Heaton/Science Photo Library**; p27 © **NASA/Science Photo Library**; p28-29 © **Mike Hollingshead/Science Faction/ SuperStock**; p30 © **NASA/SDO** (Sun); © **NASA, ESA, and the Hubble Heritage Team (STScI/AURA)-ESA/Hubble Collaboration** (galaxy); © **NASA, ESA, HEIC, and The Hubble Heritage Team (STScI/ AURA)** (nebula); p31 © **X-ray: NASA/CXC/SAO; Infrared: NASA/JPL-Caltech; Optical: MPIA, Calar Alto, O. Krause et al.**

Every effort has been made to trace and acknowledge ownership of copyright. If any rights have been omitted, the publishers offer to rectify this in any subsequent editions following notification.

First published in 2014 by Usborne Publishing Ltd., Usborne House, 83-85 Saffron Hill, London EC1N 8RT, England. www.usborne.com Copyright © 2014 Usborne Publishing Ltd. The name Usborne and the devices ♉☙ are Trade Marks of Usborne Publishing Ltd. All rights reserved. No part of this publication may be reproduced, stored in a retrieval system, or transmitted in any form or by any means, electronic, mechanical, photocopying, recording or otherwise without the prior permission of the publisher.
First published in America 2014. U.E.